Miranda
the Castaway

Miranda the Castaway

James Mayhew

Orion
Children's Books

Miranda the Castaway was originally published in 1996
by Orion Children's Books
This edition first published in Great Britain in 2014
by Orion Children's Books
a division of the Orion Publishing Group Ltd
Orion House
5 Upper Saint Martin's Lane
London WC2H 9EA
An Hachette UK Company

1 3 5 7 9 10 8 6 4 2

The Orion Publishing Group's policy is to use papers
that are natural, renewable and recyclable products and made
from wood grown in sustainable forests. The logging and
manufacturing processes are expected to conform to
the environmental regulations of the country of origin.

A catalogue record for this book
is available from the British Library.

ISBN 978 1 4440 1420 4

Printed and bound in China

www.orionbooks.co.uk

For Judith,
with thanks.

Miranda was shipwrecked.

She was cast
away on a desert
island all by herself.

She waited to be rescued,
but no one came.

Miranda didn't know what she
was supposed to do.

13

The sharks knew what to do.

Miranda watched them eat fish.

She watched the
turtles eat seaweed,
the birds eat fruit, the
snakes eat birds, and
the monkeys eat nuts.

Miranda wanted some food and water. But seawater was too salty.

And the pools were full of
insects.

At last she found a spring with clean fresh water and she drank some.

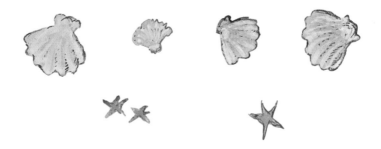

Miranda took the braces
off her teeth, tied them to a
shoelace and caught a fish.

But she couldn't bear to eat it,
and threw it back into the sea.

Then Miranda wondered if there was any fruit she could eat. She found mangoes and starfruit, bananas and monkey nuts. She ate lots of them.

By now Miranda was tired and wanted to go to sleep.

All the animals had a home or a nest. But Miranda had nowhere to go.

Miranda tried to sleep on
the beach under the stars,
but it was cold, and the
sounds of the sea and the
island kept her awake.

So the next morning, Miranda
decided to build a house of her
own.

She thought she would be safest in a tree. She used logs to make a floor.

She found leaves and tied
them together with vines to
make the walls. She filled the
gaps with mud.

She magnified the sun with
her glasses and started a fire.

It would keep her warm at
night and be useful for cooking.

It was hard work fetching
water. Miranda found hollow
sticks like straws.

She used them to carry clean
water to the treehouse.

Every day Miranda found new
things to eat on the island.

She used shells to eat off.

Coconuts to drink from.

She pulled threads from
the vine to use as string.

She made necklaces with
stones and shells, a sunhat
out of leaves.

She planted seeds and
grew flowers and vegetables
in her garden.

Miranda built more and more.
She built a bedroom, a kitchen,

a bathroom,
even a toilet.

Miranda was having fun
on the island. No school, no
bedtime, definitely no bath and
hairwash night. It seemed she
had everything she needed.

One day she saw a ship, and
she waved and shouted. But
nobody saw her because she was
so small.

Miranda waited for the ship to
come back. But it never did.

Miranda felt lonely.

The sharks had each other.

The turtles had a big family.

So did the monkeys and all
the other animals.

Even the spiders had a family.

She tried to make
friends with them.
It wasn't the same.

So Miranda built a raft.

She was sad to leave her
garden and her treehouse.

But she didn't belong on the
island.

It was time to go home.

What are you going to read next?

Have more adventures with
Horrid Henry,

or save the day with Anthony Ant!

Become a
superhero with Monstar,

float off to
sea with
Algy,

or have your very own *Pirates' Picnic.*

Grow carrots with

Lottie and Dottie,

make magic with
The Witch Dog,

and cast a spell with
The Three Little Magicians.

Enjoy all the Early Readers.

the
orion star